Isobel's Tree

Written and Illustrated by Dawn Potter

Photography by Ingrid Karolewski
(www.ingridkarolewski.com)

HELLO
my name is

Written & Illustrated By:
Dawn Potter

Photography By: Ingrid Karolewski

Eloquent Books

Eloquent Books
An imprint of Strategic Book Group
P.O. Box 333
Durham CT 06422
www.StrategicBookGroup.com

ISBN: 978-1-60860-966-6

Printed in the United States of America

For Isobel, my little gardener in training.

Special thanks to Amanda Johnson, for
unconditional support;
Tiffany Pratt and Glitter Pie Art Studio,
for whimsical enthusiasm and "good ideas"
(www.glitterpie.ca);
Ingrid Karolewski, for your ingenious eye
(www.ingridkarolewski.com);
Patricia Butler, for insightful perspective.

Isobel, do you see that tree?

That tree right there

is for you and me.

We will plant it in the ground
and watch it grow;

in the rain,

the sun,

the wind,

and the snow.

You will grow tall, and so will the tree.

Let's make a promise to go back someday,

just you and me.

When I am old, and you have grown;
you can always come back to see
the tree at our home.

Our tree will always be there,
forever and ever,
as a reminder to us that we planted
it together.

LaVergne, TN USA
20 April 2010
179899LV00002B